THESE HANDS

For Joe
And my best beloved Rodger, Kammy, Isaac & Eliza
—M.M.

For Errol
—F.C.

The text of this book is set in Adobe Jensen Pro.
The illustrations are oil wash with kneaded erasers.

The Library of Congress has cataloged the hardcover edition as follows:
Mason, Margaret H., 1954–
These hands/written by Margaret H. Mason; and illustrated by Floyd Cooper.
p. cm.
Summary: An African American man tells his grandson about a time when, despite all the
wonderful things his hands could do, they could not touch bread at the Wonder Bread factory.
Based on stories of bakery union workers; includes historical note.
[1. Civil rights—Fiction. 2. African Americans—Fiction. 3. Grandfathers—Fiction.
4. Hand—Fiction.] I. Cooper, Floyd, ill.
II. Title
PZ.M4138Th2011
[E] –dc22
2010006782

ISBN: 978-0-547-21566-2 hardcover
ISBN: 978-0-544-55546-4 paperback

Manufactured in China
SCP 10 9 8 7 6 5 4 3

4500629148

THESE HANDS

Written *by* **Margaret H. Mason**

Illustrated *by* **Floyd Cooper**

Houghton Mifflin Harcourt
Boston New York

Look at these hands, Joseph.

Did you know these hands
used to tie a triple bowline knot
in three seconds flat?

Well, I can still help a young fellow
learn to tie his shoes
—yes, I can.

Look at these hands, Joseph.

Did you know these hands
used to make the ivories sing
like a sparrow in springtime?

Well, I can still show a young fellow
how to play "Heart and Soul"
—yes, I can.

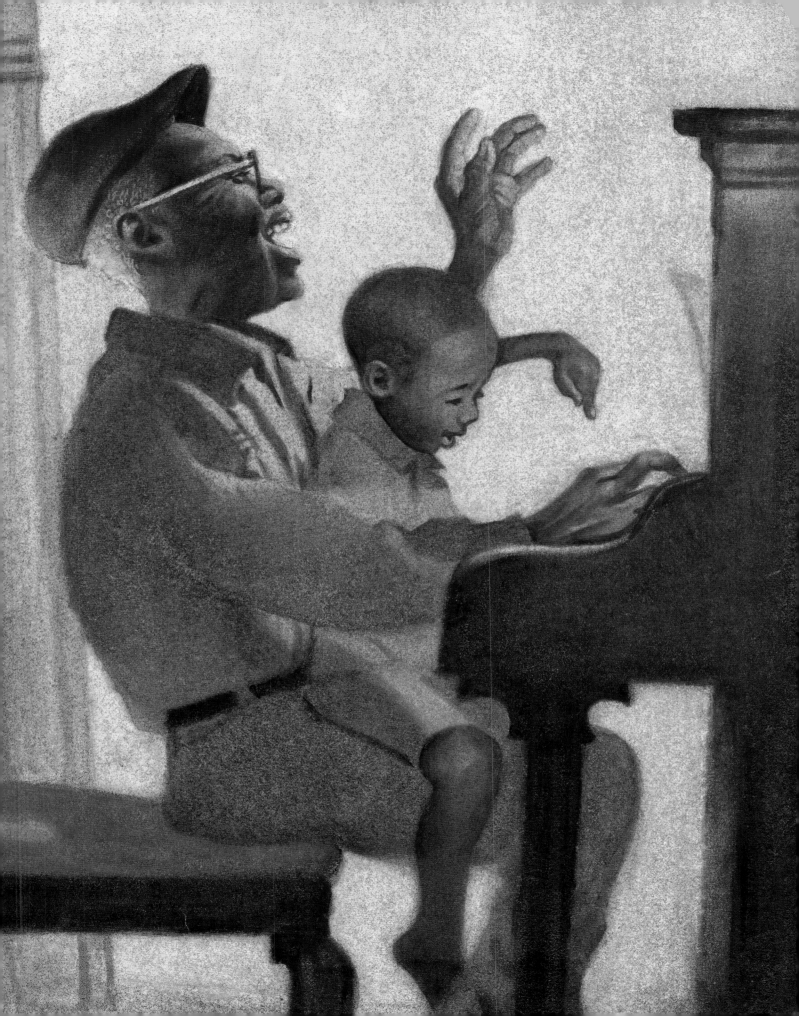

Look at these hands, Joseph.

Did you know these hands
used to pluck the ace of spades
right out of thin air?

Well, I can still teach a young fellow
how to do a waterfall shuffle
—yes, I can.

Look at these hands, Joseph.

Did you know these hands
used to throw a curve ball
faster than a dive-bombing honeybee?

Well, I can still help a young fellow
learn to hit a line drive
—yes, I can.

Look at these hands, Joseph.

Did you know these hands
were not allowed to mix
the bread dough
in the Wonder Bread factory?

Did you know these hands
were not allowed to touch
the bread dough
in the Wonder Bread factory?

These hands were only allowed
to sweep the floors
and work the line
and load the trucks.

Because the bosses said
white people would not want to eat bread
touched by these hands.

Well, these hands joined with other hands.

And we wrote our petitions,

and we carried our signs,

and we raised our voices together.

Now any hands can mix the bread dough,
no matter their color.

Now any hands can touch the bread dough, no matter their color. Yes, they can.

Look at these hands, Grandpa.
These hands used to not be able to tie a shoe,

or play the piano,

or shuffle the cards,

or hit the ball.

Now I can do all that.
Plus bake a fine loaf of bread, can't I?

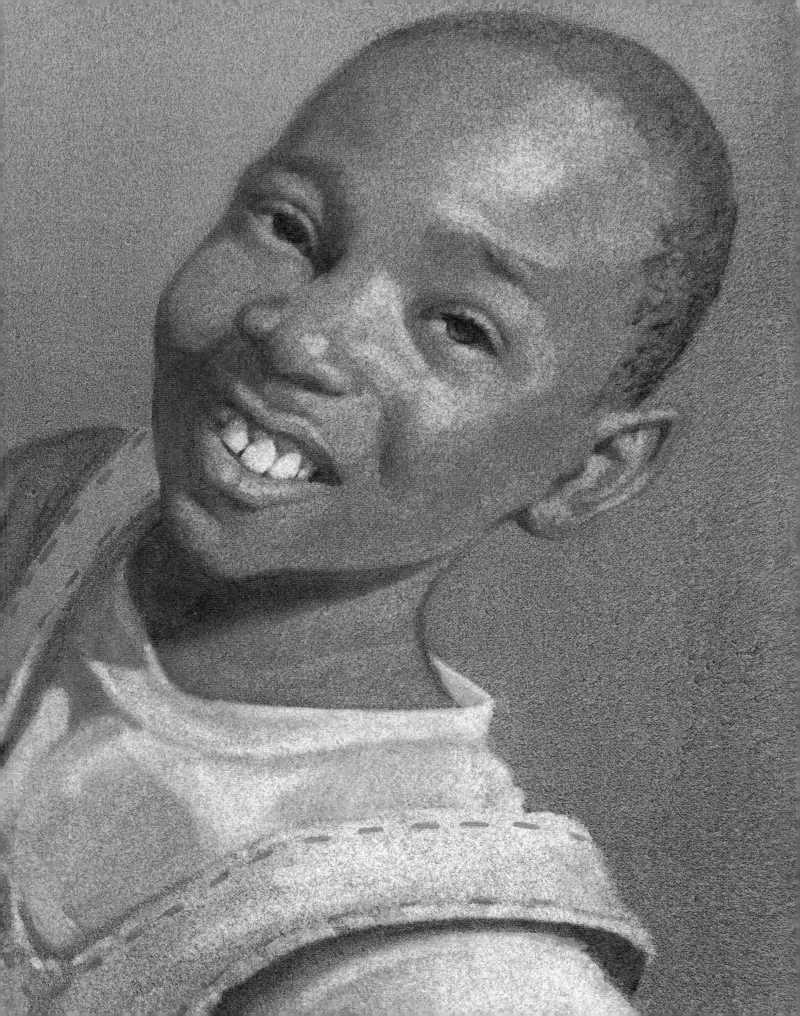

Why, yes, you can, Joseph.

Look at those hands.
Those hands can do anything.
Anything at all in this whole wide world.

Yes, you can.

Author's note

Not so long ago, during the 1950s and early 1960s, the African American workers at the Wonder Bread, Awrey, and Tastee bakery factories were allowed to sweep the floors, load the trucks, and fix the machines—but they were not allowed to work as bread dough mixers or bread dough handlers.

I learned this history from Joe Barnett, an old friend and leader of one of the bakery labor unions, which are groups of workers that join together to fight for fair treatment in their jobs. Joe told me the story one evening as we were driving to a Detroit Pistons basketball game, and I can still picture his hands gesturing, and trembling, in the crisscrossing glow of headlights. My husband, who is a labor union attorney, has also heard bakery union members talk many times over the years about these "unwritten rules" for African American workers.

A lot of what we know about how people were treated in the past comes through the retelling of stories like Joe's, or "oral history." Fellow Michigan author Jean Alicia Elster remembers her mother telling her that African American women were not allowed to try on the hats in Hudson's department store. The father of the first African American governor of New York, David Paterson, remembers being paid by the people he worked for to not attend holiday parties in the 1940s.

This history is shocking today to many people. But back then, it wasn't news; it was just how things were. In fact, newspaper ads for jobs back then often mentioned "white only" or "no colored." Deciding what jobs people could do based on their skin color was not against the law until the Civil Rights Act was passed in 1964. Before then, people may have thought such behavior was wrong, but they couldn't force other people to change.

One day in 2006, a few years after Joe died, I was watching my daughter play the violin and thinking about hands. I thought of Joe's hands, and also of his heart. And I wrote down his story.